Helme Heine

Mollywoop

Translated by Ralph Manheim

Farrar, Straus and Giroux   New York

Mollywoop

Mollywoop is in the country
Yet it's known to all and sundry.

We know the house, the fence, the tree
And now we'll meet the friends all three.

For when you're in a nasty spot
Money may not help a lot,
But a faithful friend or two
Will be much more use to you.

Cycling

A bike, unless you keep it clean,
Will rust and won't be worth a bean.

And when you want to take a trip,
You have to blow the tires up.

The three friends jump on board and ride
Through puddles long and deep and wide.

The Concert

Music is bothersome indeed,
  'Specially when you're trying to read.

But even worse is listening
And hearing not a single thing.

The Archery Contest

To Mollywoop the archers come
To shoot the target and have fun.

Fat Percy stands and plies the bow;
The arrow's Charlie Boy, you know.

And Johnny steers him, makes him fly
Directly to the black bull's-eye.

The one who gets the most bull's-eyes
Is king and wins the biggest prize.

Superstars

When Johnny enters on the scene,
The girls they all begin to scream.

No wonder Charlie Rooster's vain,
They've cast him as the weathervane.

And fat Percy's silky twirl
Once featured as Napoleon's curl.

Dressing Up

They say that clothes have made the man—
Or woman—since the world began.

Fat Percy here you see as bride
Although he's somewhat short and wide.

And here's King Charlie on his horse;
He's strong and brave and good, of course.

A black top hat is Johnny's whim;
He says the size is right for him.

Night Life

The three friends find it quite a lark
Making whoopee after dark.

But rising early with the sun
Isn't nearly so much fun.

Indians

When playing Indians they wear
A lot of feathers in their hair.

Their painted skins and warlike sounds
Scare all the folk for miles around.

When Joe the tomcat heard the din,
He told the friends to pack it in.
To punish him they tied him tight
And left him standing there all night.

Bath Day

Bath day makes fat Percy mope,
He hates the water and the soap.

Charlie's filling up the tub,
And Johnny's standing by to scrub.

With Charlie dousing him in drink
Our Percy's turning very pink.

At last the mud is off his skin,
So happily he rolls back in.

Charlie Rooster

When lightning flashes and it pours,
Our Charlie rushes out of doors.

For Charlie Rooster is quite vain
And looks his best in pouring rain.

He is a most impressive sight,
The chickens cackle with delight.

But if it rains too hard and long,
Our Charlie's plumage looks all wrong.

Paradise

In Mollywoop there is a closet
With scrumptious delicacies in it:

Spaghetti, chocolate, marmalade,
Salami, cheese, and lemonade.

There's charlotte russe and flavored ice,
Et cetera—a paradise.

But in the corner there's a trap.
Fat Percy's tail goes in—and snap!

The Visit

In case you have no dime to spend
For cake and coffee, meet a friend.

And if you pick him a bouquet,
He'll stop and pass the time of day.

A parting kiss, though, at the end
Is never sad between two friends.
You'll meet again and find it's true
That he's picked a bouquet for you!